# FANTASTIC FRUITS

## A GRIMAL GROVE COLORING BOOK

Charlesbridge

Ralph Masiello

To the lumpy, oddly shaped, strangely colored, unusual, and amazingly beautiful rare fruits out there, all looking for someone to discover and love them.—R. M.

I dedicate this book to my wonderful and devoted husband, "JO," and my three fabulous children, Gabrielle, Charlotte, and Jackson. Thank you for always believing in me and encouraging me to live my dream.—K. L.-O.

To my daughters, Ana and Zoe: The fruits of my labor pale in comparison to the purpose you bestow upon me.—P. G.

At the time of publication, all URLs printed in this book were accurate and active. Charlesbridge and the author are not responsible for the content or accessibility of any website.

Photo credit for Karen Ludwig-O'Leary by Tony Gregory

Published by Charlesbridge
85 Main Street, Watertown, MA 02472
(617) 926-0329
www.charlesbridge.com

ISBN 978-1-62354-141-5
Printed in China
(pb) 10 9 8 7 6 5 4 3 2 1

Printed by 1010 Printing International Limited in Huizhou, Guangdong, China
Production supervision by Brian G. Walker
Designed by Jacqueline N. Cote

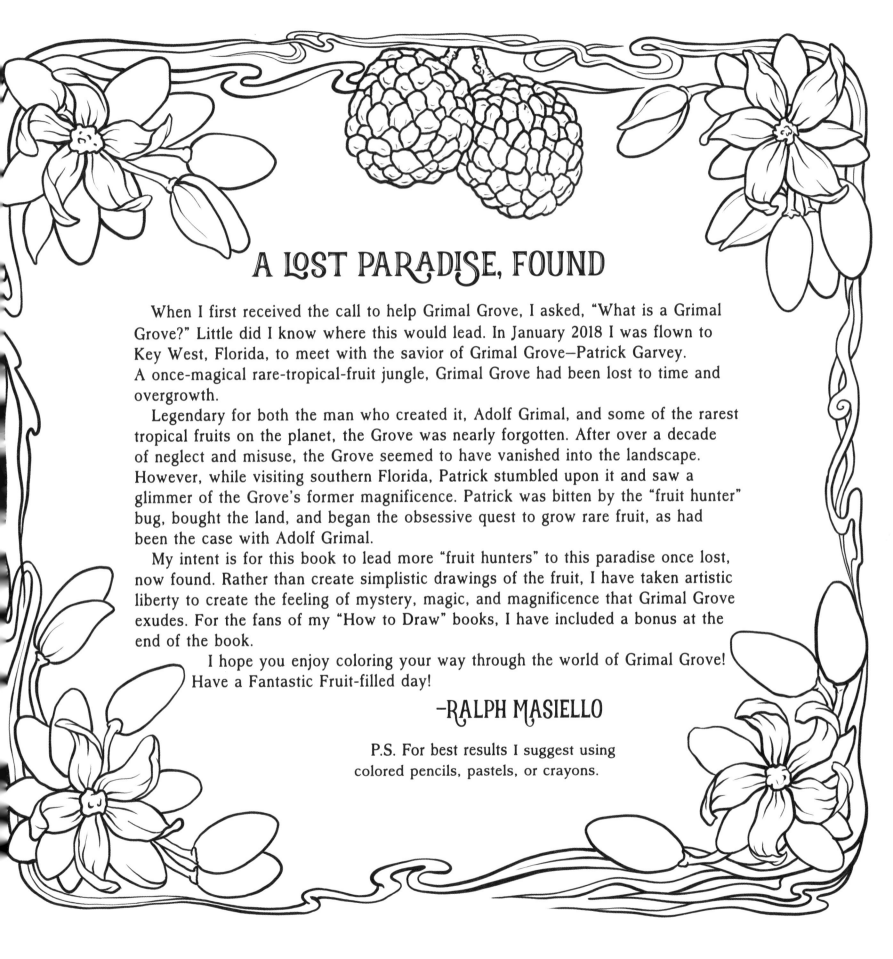

# A LOST PARADISE, FOUND

When I first received the call to help Grimal Grove, I asked, "What is a Grimal Grove?" Little did I know where this would lead. In January 2018 I was flown to Key West, Florida, to meet with the savior of Grimal Grove—Patrick Garvey. A once-magical rare-tropical-fruit jungle, Grimal Grove had been lost to time and overgrowth.

Legendary for both the man who created it, Adolf Grimal, and some of the rarest tropical fruits on the planet, the Grove was nearly forgotten. After over a decade of neglect and misuse, the Grove seemed to have vanished into the landscape. However, while visiting southern Florida, Patrick stumbled upon it and saw a glimmer of the Grove's former magnificence. Patrick was bitten by the "fruit hunter" bug, bought the land, and began the obsessive quest to grow rare fruit, as had been the case with Adolf Grimal.

My intent is for this book to lead more "fruit hunters" to this paradise once lost, now found. Rather than create simplistic drawings of the fruit, I have taken artistic liberty to create the feeling of mystery, magic, and magnificence that Grimal Grove exudes. For the fans of my "How to Draw" books, I have included a bonus at the end of the book.

I hope you enjoy coloring your way through the world of Grimal Grove! Have a Fantastic Fruit-filled day!

## –RALPH MASIELLO

P.S. For best results I suggest using
colored pencils, pastels, or crayons.

BANANA

SAPODILLA

BREADFRUIT

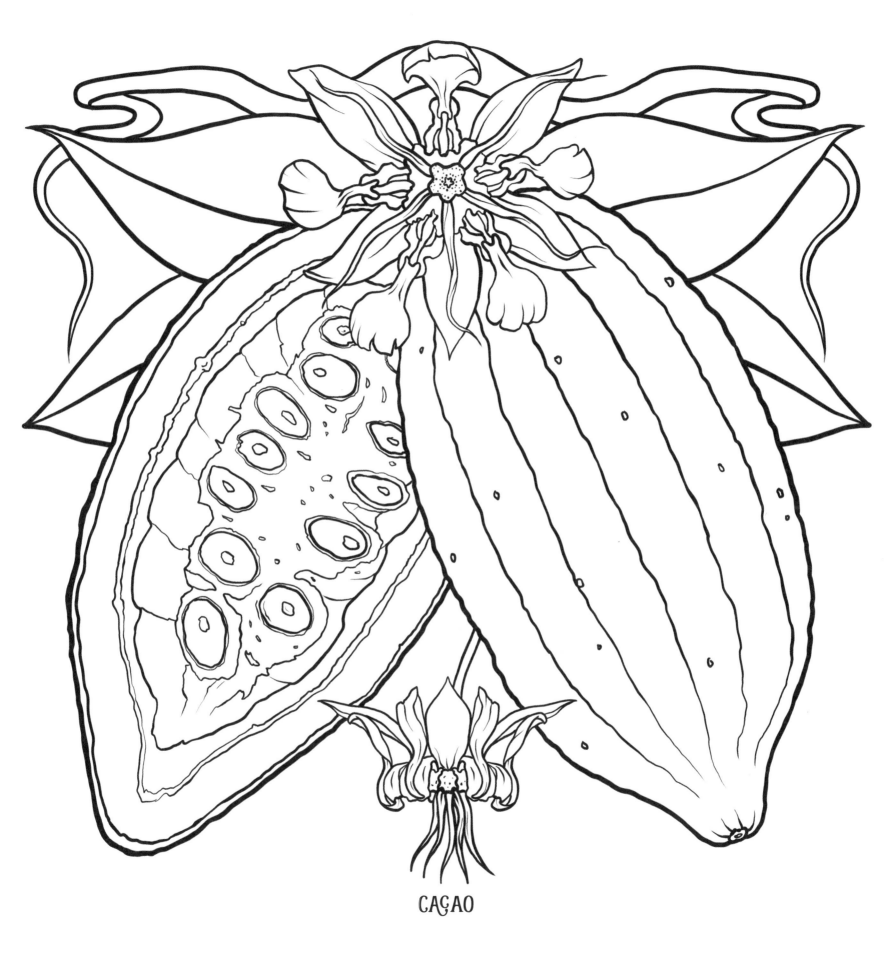

CACAO

SURINAM CHERRY

CHERIMOYA

CARAMBOLA

JABOTICABA

DRAGON FRUIT

SOURSOP

PAPAYÁ

BILIMBI

WHITE SAPOTE

AVOCADO

WAX JAMBU

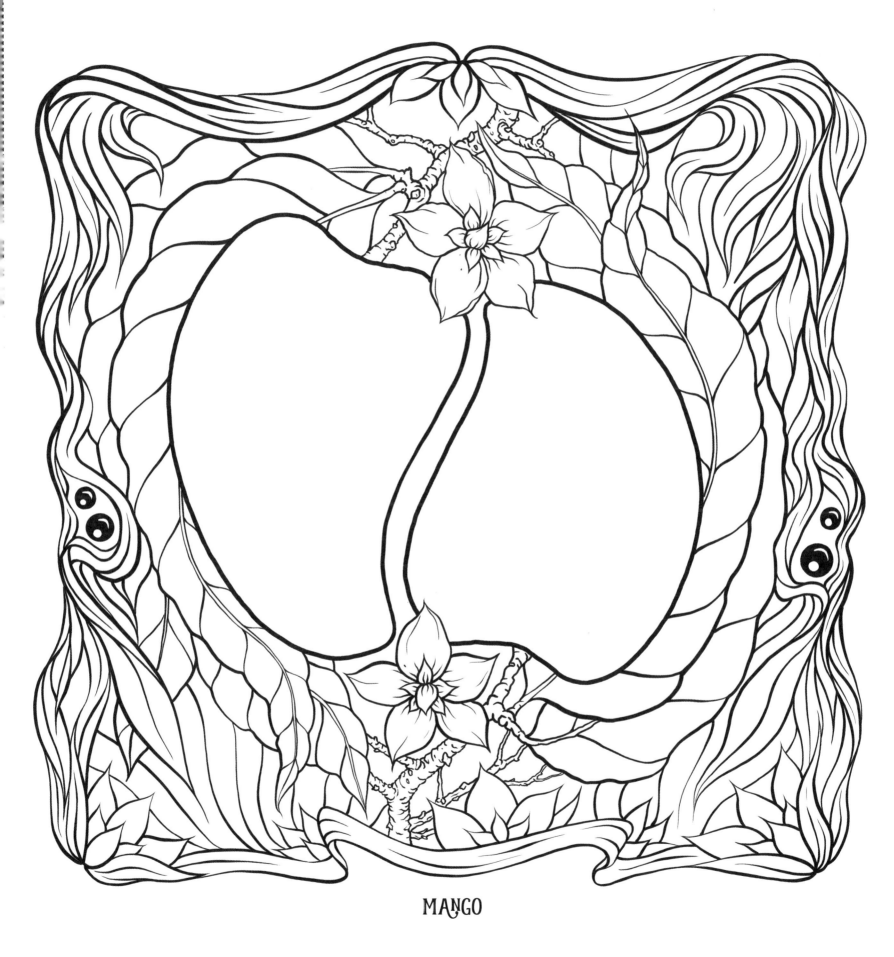

MANGO

CANISTEL AND BARBADOS CHERRIES

JACKFRUIT

MANGOSTEEN

DURIAN

GUAVA

RAMBUTAN

ALUPAG AND MAMEY SAPOTE

LYCHEES AND LONGANS

# HOW TO DRAW A DRAGON FRUIT

## FOLLOW THE STEPS IN GRAY.

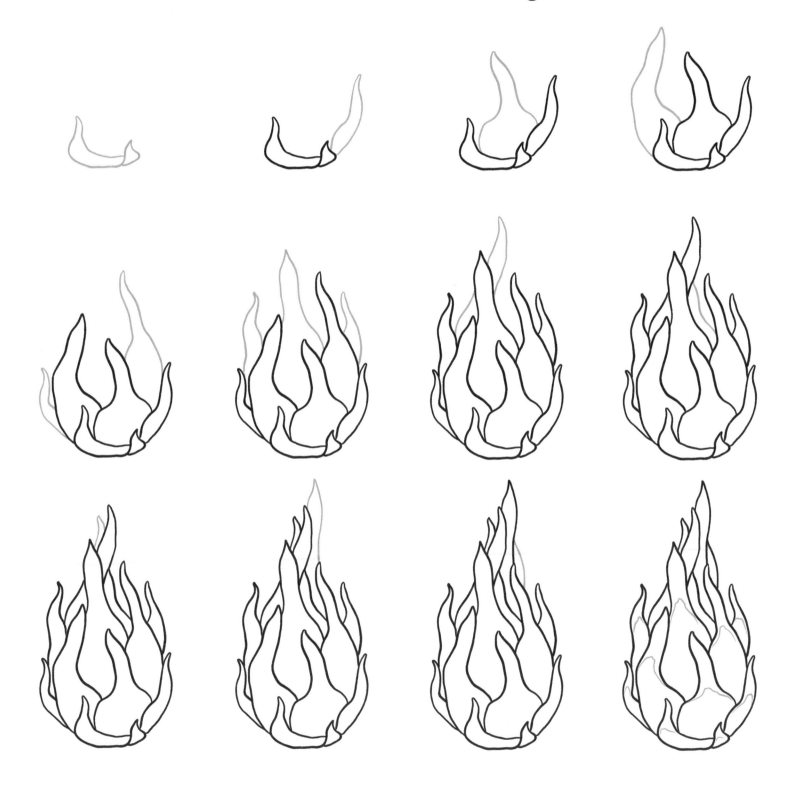

# HOW TO DRAW A DRAGON FRUIT DRAGON

## TURN THE DRAGON FRUIT UPSIDE DOWN!

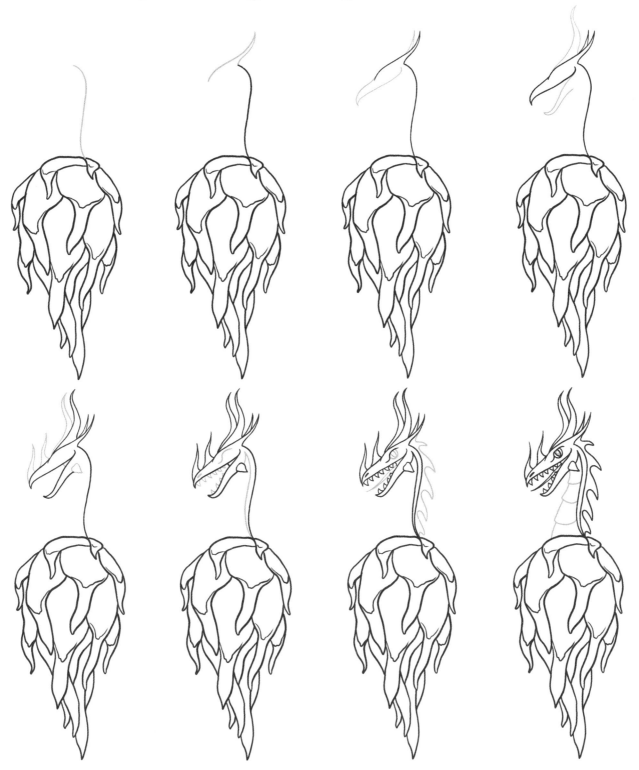

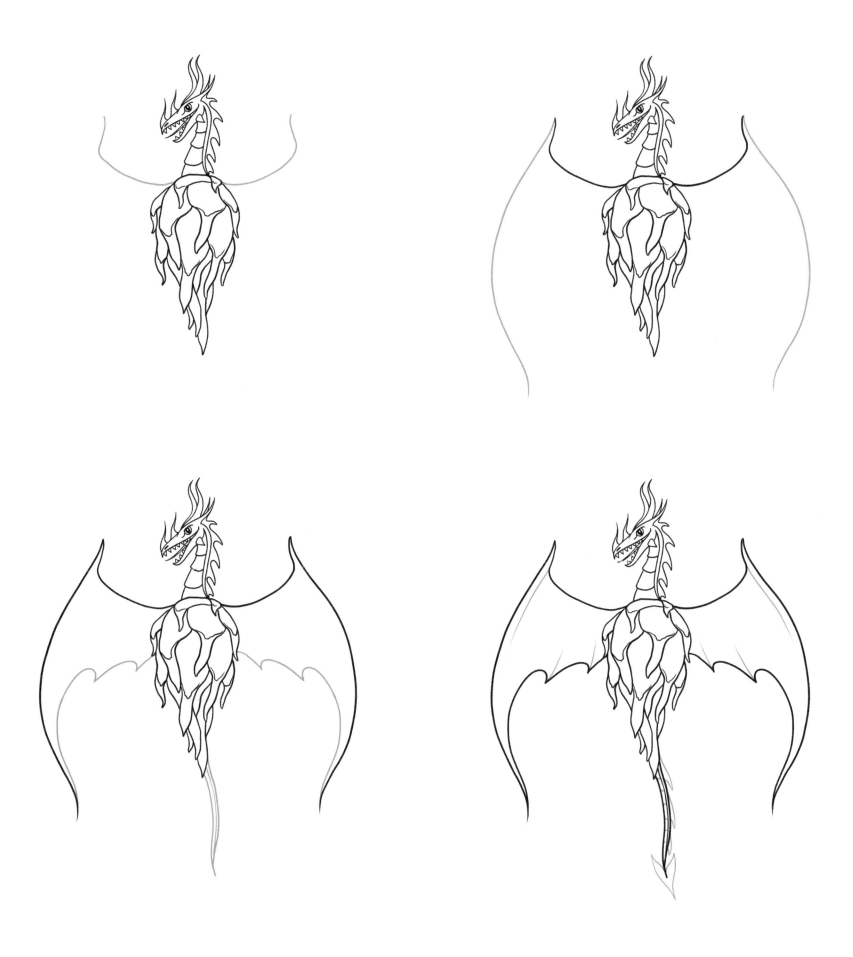

DRAGON FRUIT DRAGON

# GRIMAL GROVE NEEDS YOUR HELP!

Learn more about Grimal Grove and the Growing Hope Initiative.
http://www.grimalgrove.com and https://www.growinghopeinitiative.org

Growing Hope Initiative channel on YouTube:
   https://www.youtube.com/channel/UC_ScCASlYCqjHoENmUiqdmA

Learn more about the man who had the dream: Adolf Grimal.
Garvey, Patrick. "Old Man and the Grove." Uploaded November 15, 2016. YouTube video.
   https://www.youtube.com/watch?v=pAiNrHpUI6E

# LEARN MORE ABOUT RARE TROPICAL FRUITS:

## WEBSITES

**Preston B. Bird and Mary Heinlein Fruit & Spice Park**
https://redlandfruitandspice.com
Learn about this tropical botanical garden with over five hundred varieties of fruits, vegetables, spices, herbs, and nuts.

**Fairchild Tropical Botanic Garden**
https://www.fairchildgarden.org
Learn about the conservation of tropical plants.

**FruitScapes**
https://trec.ifas.ufl.edu/fruitscapes
Resources on how to plant and grow fruit trees.

**National Tropical Botanical Garden Breadfruit Institute**
https://ntbg.org/breadfruit
Learn about the uses of breadfruit for food and reforestation.

## BOOKS ABOUT RARE FRUIT

Blancke, Rolf. *Tropical Fruits and Other Edible Plants of the World: An Illustrated Guide.* Ithaca, NY: Comstock Publishing Associates, 2016.

Gollner, Adam L. *The Fruit Hunters: A Story of Nature, Adventure, Commerce, and Obsession.* New York: Scribner, 2008.

## MOVIES

Chang, Yung. *The Fruit Hunters.* Eye Steel Film: Documentary Film. https://www.youtube.com/watch?v=blaRgwWvIso
Driven by their intense passion, the Fruit Hunters travel the globe exploring jungles to find and try to save rare tropical fruits before it is too late.